W9-BNU-972

Dear Parent:
Your child's love of reading starts here!

Every child learns to read in a different way and at his or her own speed. Some go back and forth between reading levels and read favorite books again and again. Others read through each level in order. You can help your young reader improve and become more confident by encouraging his or her own interests and abilities. From books your child reads with you to the first books he or she reads alone, there are I Can Read Books for every stage of reading:

My First

SHARED READING
Basic language, word repetition, and whimsical illustrations, ideal for sharing with your emergent reader

1

BEGINNING READING
Short sentences, familiar words, and simple concepts for children eager to read on their own

2

READING WITH HELP
Engaging stories, longer sentences, and language play for developing readers

3

READING ALONE
Complex plots, challenging vocabulary, and high-interest topics for the independent reader

4

ADVANCED READING
Short paragraphs, chapters, and exciting themes for the perfect bridge to chapter books

I Can Read Books have introduced children to the joy of reading since 1957. Featuring award-winning authors and illustrators and a fabulous cast of beloved characters, I Can Read Books set the standard for beginning readers.

A lifetime of discovery begins with the magical words **"I Can Read!"**

Visit www.icanread.com for information on enriching your child's reading experience.

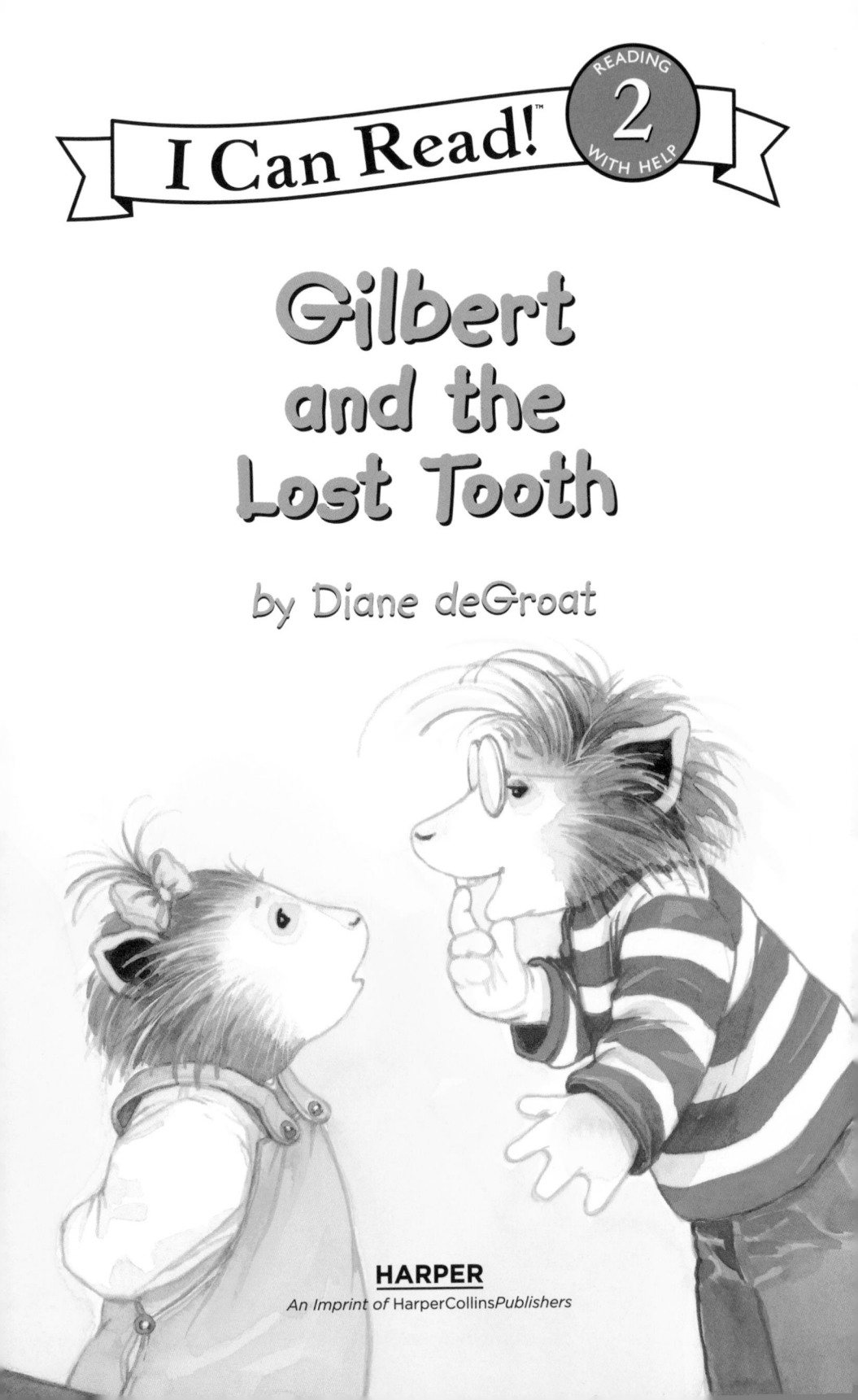
I Can Read!™
READING
2
WITH HELP
Gilbert and the Lost Tooth
by Diane deGroat
HARPER
An Imprint of HarperCollinsPublishers

To Rachel Funk
and her brilliant students

I Can Read Book® is a trademark of HarperCollins Publishers.

Gilbert and the Lost Tooth Copyright © 2012 by Diane deGroat All rights reserved. No part of this book may be used or reproduced in any manner whatsoever without written permission except in the case of brief quotations embodied in critical articles and reviews.
Manufactured in China. For information address HarperCollins Children's Books, a division of HarperCollins Publishers, 195 Broadway, New York, NY 10007.
www.icanread.com

Library of Congress Cataloging-in-Publication Data is available.
ISBN 978-0-06-125214-3 (trade bdg.) — ISBN 978-0-06-125216-7 (pbk.)

17 18 SCP 10 9 8 7 6 5 ❖ First Edition

Contents

Chapter 1:
The Wiggles 6

Chapter 2:
The Worries 13

Chapter 3:
The Wake-up 22

Chapter 1: The Wiggles

Gilbert had a loose tooth.

It wiggled during spelling.

It wobbled when he walked.

And it hurt when he bit into

his sandwich.

"Maybe it will fall out today,"
Patty said.
"Don't forget to put it
under your pillow if it does."
Patty smiled.
She had a big window in her mouth.
Frank and Margaret had windows too.

Lewis didn't have a window
in his mouth.
Lewis didn't even have a loose tooth.
He didn't want to hear about teeth.
He wanted to play kickball.

"Gilbert!" Lewis shouted.

"It's your turn.

Stop playing with your tooth

and kick the ball!"

Gilbert kicked, but he missed
and fell on his bottom!
"Uh-oh!" he said, holding his mouth.
"My tooth came out!"
Patty said, "Yay, Gilbert!
Now the tooth fairy will come."
Lewis didn't say, "Yay!"
He said, "Gilbert, stop playing
with your tooth and kick the ball!"
Gilbert put the tooth into his pocket.
Then he kicked the ball
and made a run.
Everyone said, "Yay!"
Except Lewis.

When the bell rang,

Lewis picked up the kickball.

He picked up the soccer ball.

He picked up the baseball.

And he picked up something

small and white.

Chapter 2: The Worries

After school, Gilbert ran home.

"My tooth fell out!" he shouted.

"Let me see it," Lola said.

Gilbert reached into his pocket.

But he didn't find a tooth.

He found a hole!

Gilbert ran to Mother and cried,

"I lost my tooth!"

Mother smiled and said,

"It's about time, Gilbert.

It was very loose."

"No," Gilbert said.

"I mean I REALLY lost my tooth.

I can't find it!

I can't put it under my pillow!"

Mother said, "Hmmm . . .

Maybe you can leave

a note for the Tooth Fairy

to tell her what happened."

"I'm going to leave a note too,"
Lola said.
"Maybe the Tooth Fairy
will bring me something."
"But you didn't lose a tooth,"
Gilbert said.
"She doesn't know that," Lola said.

Gilbert wrote a note.

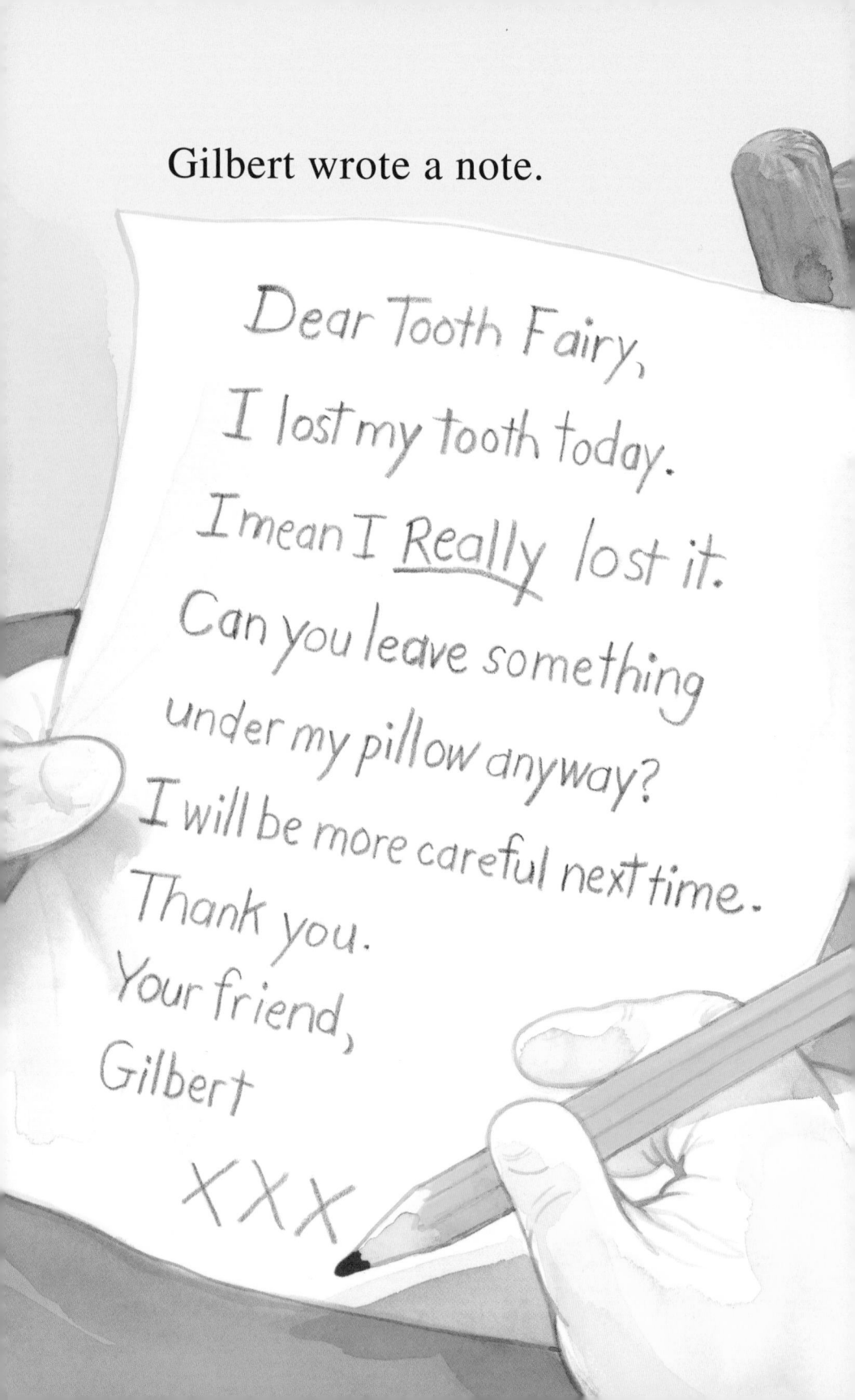

Lola wrote a note too.

That night, Gilbert put the note under his pillow.

Lola put her note under her pillow.

And Lewis put a small white tooth under his pillow.

Chapter 3: The Wake-up

When the sun went down
and the moon came up,
the Tooth Fairy went to work.
She packed her bag full of gifts
and money.
She turned on her magic tooth-detector
and flew into the night.
She flew over the rooftops
until her tooth-detector lit up.
When she was right over Lewis's house,
it grew brighter and brighter!
"I found one!" she said.

She crept into Lewis's room and
peeked under his pillow.
She found a small white tooth.
"My tooth-detector is always right!"
she said.
But before she put the tooth
into her bag, she looked at it closely.

Then she looked at Lewis snoring
with his mouth open.
"Hmmm . . . ," she said.
Suddenly the tooth-detector buzzed
and beeped like crazy.
It was pointing toward Gilbert's house!

The next morning, Gilbert looked under his pillow and found money! Mother said, "The Tooth Fairy must have seen your note, Gilbert." Gilbert put the money into his piggy bank.

Lola looked under her pillow.
She found a pink toothbrush.
Mother said, "The Tooth Fairy
must want you to take care
of your teeth, Lola."
Lola brushed her teeth very hard.
Maybe they would come loose!

Lewis looked under his pillow.

He didn't find money.

He didn't find a toothbrush.

He found a note that said:

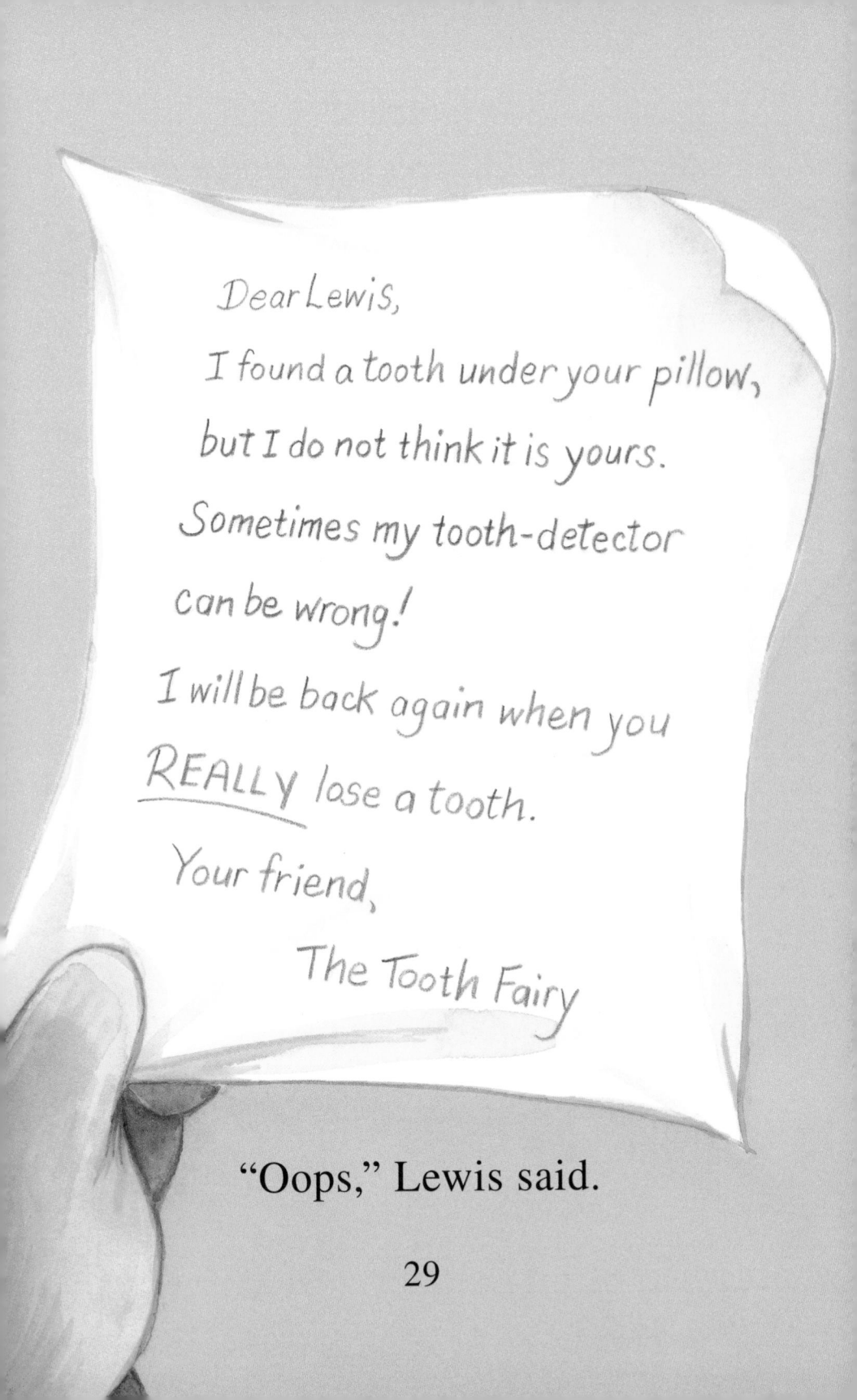

"Oops," Lewis said.

At recess, Gilbert told everyone about the note he had left under his pillow.

Lewis wondered if he should tell
everyone about the tooth
he had found on the playground.
He wondered so hard that he
didn't see the ball coming.
It hit him right in the face!

"OW!" Lewis cried.

But then he felt something

wiggly and wobbly in his mouth.

"My tooth is loose!" he shouted.

Everyone said, "Yay!"

Even Lewis.